THE  ™

 S0-CWQ-047

with FRANKIE FUMBLE in

FOOTBALL FRIENDS

Sport Mites™ characters created
and drawn by Bob Pelkowski

Text by Alias Smith

BARRON'S
New York • London • Toronto • Sydney

ISBN 0-8120-4242-5
PRINTED IN HONG KONG

Sport Mite Frankie Fumble was having an argument
with his big brother Joe—and Frankie was losing.
"Listen," said Joe. "You *can't* go with me,
you're not ready for a real football game yet."
"I can play," argued Frankie. "I know about
football. I've even got my equipment on."

"Next week maybe, O.K.?" Joe promised half-heartedly, as he raced down the porch steps, almost knocking Frankie over.

"I want to go now . . ." bellowed Frankie.

Frankie stomped down the steps. He watched Joe disappear through the trees into the nearby park.

"Come on, pal," Frankie said to his football.
"Let's go over to the Mitey Clubhouse. We can always
have fun playing football with our friends the Sport
Mites—even if it isn't in a real game, and Redbert
will be there. He knows how to help a Sport Mite."

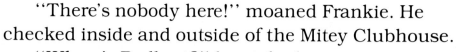

"There's nobody here!" moaned Frankie. He
checked inside and outside of the Mitey Clubhouse.
"Where's Redbert?" he sighed.
The moment Frankie mentioned Redbert's name,
a magic calmness filled the air.

Frankie saw a streak of red glide across the sparkling blue sky. Redbert, friend and mascot of all the Sport Mites, winged his way downward and landed on the crossbar between the goalposts in the field beside the Mitey Clubhouse.

"Redbert! Redbert!" Frankie cried as he dashed across the field.

"My big brother . . . (puff) said I wasn't ready . . . (puff) to play a real game . . ."

The story tumbled out as Frankie ran.

"Slow down, Sport Mite," the bright red bird said. "Sounds like you're disappointed you couldn't go with your brother."

"You said it, Redbert!"

"Does this mean you'll stop liking football?" Redbert asked.

"NEVER!! Football is my favorite sport."

"Good! Because I happen to have a real football game lined up here tomorrow between the Sport Mites and the Visitors. Will you help me get the field ready?" Redbert asked Frankie.

"A real game!" Frankie shouted. "For sure!"

Frankie gently placed his football near the goalpost. "I'm ready, Redbert!"

"What can we use to get the field ready for the game?" Frankie thought.

At midfield, he made a pile: a bag of chalk dust, a clock, orange crates, planks, a chair, a piece of chalk, a chalkboard, a square piece of wood, string, a stick and a pail full of pebbles.

"Let's see what you've got there," said Redbert.

"I'll start with the orange crates," Frankie said importantly. "A football team has eleven players. They need a place to sit. Two crates and a plank make a good players' bench. One is for the Sport Mites . . . that's us! And the other is for the Visitors."

"This crate is a table," Frankie continued. He arranged the square piece of wood, clock, chair, chalkboard, and piece of chalk.

"See! It's for the timer and scorekeeper."

"It looks good so far," nodded Redbert, "Do you remember what the timer and scorekeeper do during the game?"

"Sure I do," said Frankie. "The scorekeeper marks the points on the chalkboard. The team with the most points wins. Running or passing the ball over the other team's goal line is a touchdown, and you get six points. Kicking the ball through the goalposts after a touchdown is an extra point. Kicking the ball through the goalposts during regular play is a field goal and you get three points. You have to do everything well . . . run, pass, and kick . . . to win at football!"

"What about the timer?" asked Redbert.

"That's easy," said Frankie. "Each team has sixty minutes to make points. The timer keeps track of the quarters and halves in the game. A quarter means fifteen minutes in football. There are four quarters in a game, two in each half."

Frankie brought the pail of pebbles over to the goal line.
"Now I'll mark the boundaries of the field with chalk dust.
You put a pebble every ten yards, Redbert, starting at the goal
line. You'll need ten pebbles, because a football field is 100
yards long. I'll tie a string to a stick at each pebble. You fly
across the field with the string and hold it on the other side,"
Frankie directed.

"Why so many lines?" asked Redbert.

Frankie snapped the chalk-covered string finishing the last neat white stripe.

"You know," said Frankie. "The team with the ball has four tries to move it ten yards."

"What if you can't go the whole ten yards?"

Frankie shook his finger at Redbert. "Then it's too bad for you—the other team gets the ball!"

"Good work," Redbert said, as he fluttered above the field to get a bird's-eye view of their efforts. "And your brother says you're not ready for a real game!"

Frankie smiled. "See you tomorrow!"

He picked up his football and gave it a pat. "You and I have a big day coming up," he said as he trudged homeward.

Early the next morning, the Sport Mites met at the Mitey Clubhouse.

"Good luck in the game today, Frankie," said Sport Mite Rodney Rebound.

"Thanks, Rodney," said Frankie who reached the players' bench just as Redbert, who was the referee, blew the whistle to begin the first quarter.

From downfield, Frankie saw the other Sport Mites in the bleachers stretching their necks to catch a glimpse of the action.

Suddenly, Frankie forgot the crowd. All he concentrated on was the football, the players . . . and the goal line!

"Three more yards for a first down," thought Frankie.
"92—26—53—HUT—HUT!" the quarterback signaled.
"Oh, boy! A hand-off to me!" Frankie grinned.
The center snapped the ball. Swiftly, the
quarterback slipped the football into Frankie's hands.

Frankie tucked the football snugly under his arm and started running. Two of the visiting players were soon on Frankie's heels. "Uh, oh! I have company," gulped Frankie, as he headed for the sideline in front of the yard marker.

"First down—Sport Mites," Redbert announced.

Frankie's team tried hard to make another first down, but after the third down they still had six yards to go. "I'll try kicking a field goal," he told his teammates in the huddle before the fourth down.

Frankie wound up and kicked with all his might.

"Field goal—Sport Mites," Redbert reported to the enthusiastic crowd.

"Now it's our turn to play defense. We have to get the football from the visitors. What will they do—pass or run?" wondered Frankie.

On the next play, he saw the Visitors' wide receiver run a pass pattern across the field.

"It's a pass for sure!" Frankie exclaimed.

Determined to get the ball, Frankie darted toward the player. The football zipped across the field. It popped in and out of the wide receiver's hands. Scrambling, Frankie dove into the growing pile of wagging arms, legs, and helmets and fell on top of the football.

"Fumble . . . Visitors. Recovery . . . Sport Mites!" crowed Redbert.

Frankie felt a burst of energy.

"Play 26, Frankie," the Sport Mites' quarterback said.

Frankie tingled with anticipation. With his eyes fixed on the goal line, Frankie took the hand-off and turned on the burners.

"Touchdown!" Redbert's voice boomed out over the rollicking cheers of the Sport Mites as Frankie raced into the end zone.

"Hurray for Frankie! Hip, hip, hurray!" the fans chanted as Frankie danced his Sport Mite Shuffle in the end zone.

Frankie got ready to place kick for the extra point. Digging into the ground with his cleats, he charged toward the football. POING! The football sailed up . . . up . . . up into the air over the crossbar between the goalposts.

"Extra point . . . Sport Mites," Redbert announced.

Frankie looked around at all the smiling faces. There was his brother Joe, cheering with all the others.

"I may not be ready for a real game with the big guys," he said to himself. "But with my Sport Mites friends, I can do anything!"

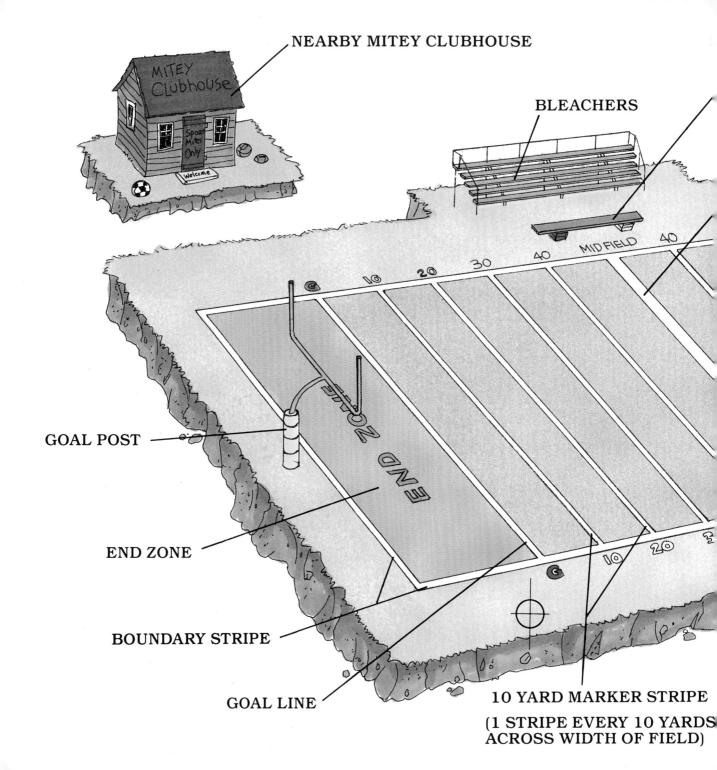

NEARBY MITEY CLUBHOUSE

MiTEY Clubhouse

Sport Mites Only

Welcome

BLEACHERS

MID FIELD

40

40

10 20 30 40

10 20

GOAL POST

END ZONE

END ZONE

BOUNDARY STRIPE

GOAL LINE

10 YARD MARKER STRIPE

(1 STRIPE EVERY 10 YARDS
ACROSS WIDTH OF FIELD)

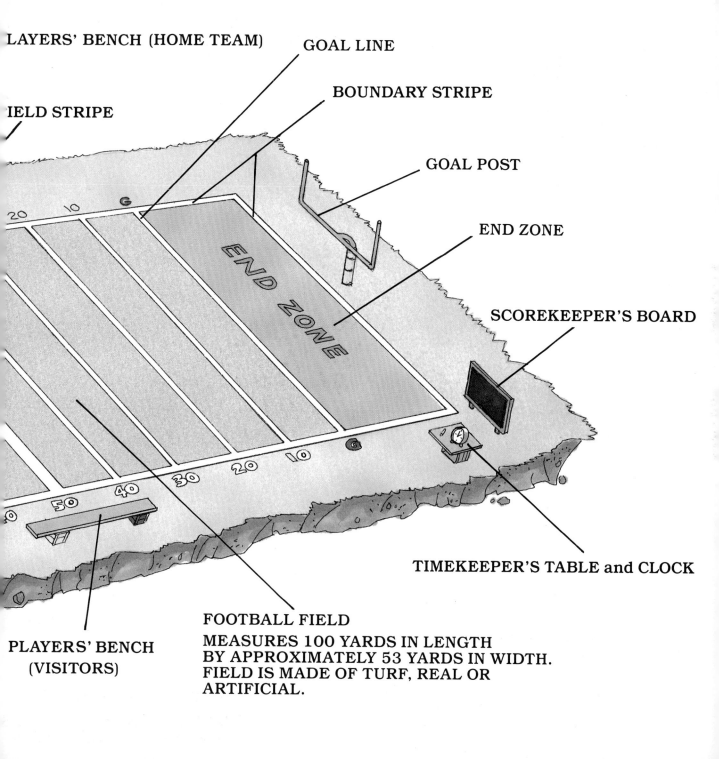

LAYERS' BENCH (HOME TEAM)

GOAL LINE

BOUNDARY STRIPE

IELD STRIPE

GOAL POST

END ZONE

SCOREKEEPER'S BOARD

TIMEKEEPER'S TABLE and CLOCK

PLAYERS' BENCH
(VISITORS)

FOOTBALL FIELD

MEASURES 100 YARDS IN LENGTH
BY APPROXIMATELY 53 YARDS IN WIDTH.
FIELD IS MADE OF TURF, REAL OR
ARTIFICIAL.

FOOTBALL TERMS

center   The player who takes the middle position on the line of scrimmage and hikes the ball.

cleats   Special shoes that have metal or plastic projections attached to the underside to prevent slipping.

defense   The act of protecting and trying to prevent the other team from scoring.

fumble   To lose control and possession of the football during play action.

goal line   The end boundary line at each end of the field. When the ball passes over your opponent's goal line, points are scored.

hand-off   The process when a player (not the center) hands the football to another teammate.

helmet   A protective head covering.

hike   When the center passes the ball between his legs to the quarterback on the line of scrimmage.

huddle   When the players crowd closely together to talk about the play action.

line of scrimmage   The place where the ball is put down and both teams face each other to start the play.

mascot   A person or animal thought to bring good luck.

pass   The process when a player throws the football to another teammate.

pass pattern   A planned passing play in which the receiver runs to a definite area to catch the football.

place kick   A kick of the football to try to score while the football is being held in place on the ground by a teammate.

quarterback   A backfield player who often calls the plays, throws the ball or hands it off.

receiver   A player who runs to catch a pass.

referee   A non-player who is in charge of the game action and enforces the rules.

recovery   Gaining control of the football after a fumble.

sideline   The side boundary of the field.